The Very Helpful Hedgehog

This edition first published in the United Kingdom in 2012 by
Pavilion Children's Books, an imprint of
Pavilion Books Company Ltd.
43 Great Ormond Street
London
WC1N 3HZ
www.pavilionbooks.com

ISBN 978-1-84365-198-7

A CIP catalogue record for this book is available from the British Library.

20 19 18 17 16 15 14 13 12

Reproduction by Dot Gradations Ltd, UK
Printed and bound by BALTOprint UAB, Lithuania

This book can be ordered directly from the publisher online at
www.pavilionbooks.com

The Very Helpful Hedgehog

Rosie Wellesley

PAVILION

Isaac the hedgehog lived a quiet life under the tree by the paddock and never spoke to anyone.

He never helped anyone and no one ever helped him. He liked it that way.

One afternoon he was feeling sleepy. He had been for a walk on his own, caught a grub and eaten it, alone.

Isaac had just settled down for a nap
in a pile of old leaves when...

THUD!

Something had landed on his back
and he couldn't get it off.

He tried to see it...

and tried again...

and tried some more...

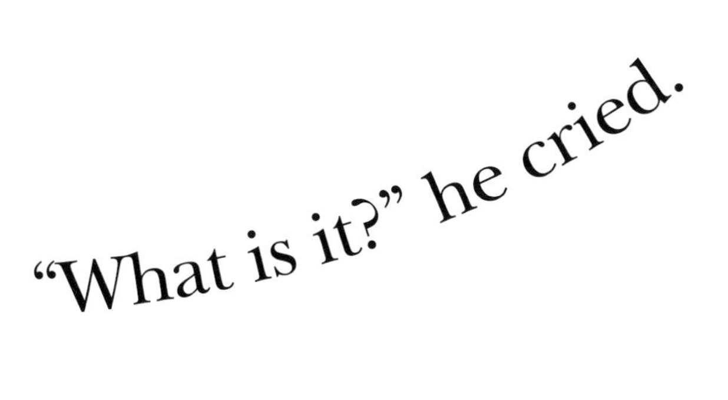

“What is it?” he cried.

He looked up.

An apple!

It must be an apple, he thought.

The apple was stuck.

The apple was very stuck.

The more Isaac tried to get it off,
the more it stuck onto his back.

Oh no, he thought,
and started to cry.
I have no one to help me!

He cried so hard he didn't hear the voice above him.

"Hmmm, an apple. At last an apple
has rolled into my paddock."

CRUNCH

"Who are you? Why were you under my apple?" asked the donkey.

"I do so love apples. That was my first in a very long time."

Isaac said nothing.

"Do you like apples? You must.
Everyone must! So sweet!
So crunchy!"

Still Isaac said nothing.

So the donkey kept talking,

"Apples with custard,
apple pie, toffee apples,
apple crumble!

Oh joy! OH JOY!"

"Gala apples,
Granny Smith,
Irish Peach,
Honey Crisp.

Golden Supreme,
Golden Delicious,
Braeburn, Bismarck, Jonalicious.

Gilpin,
Franklin,
Cindy Red,
Cox's Orange and Cat's Head.

Such feasts!
Such appley treats!
So many different types to eat!"

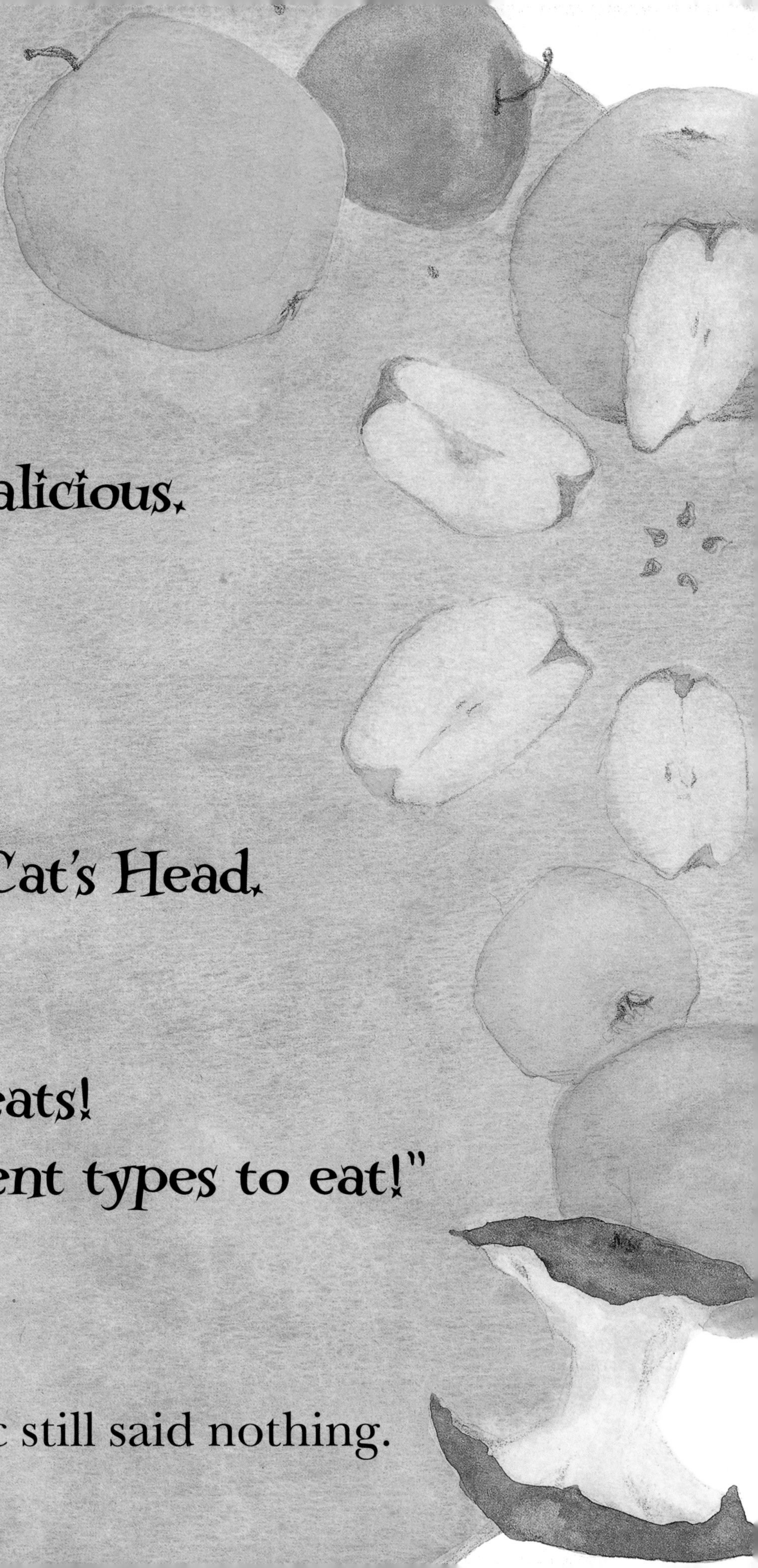

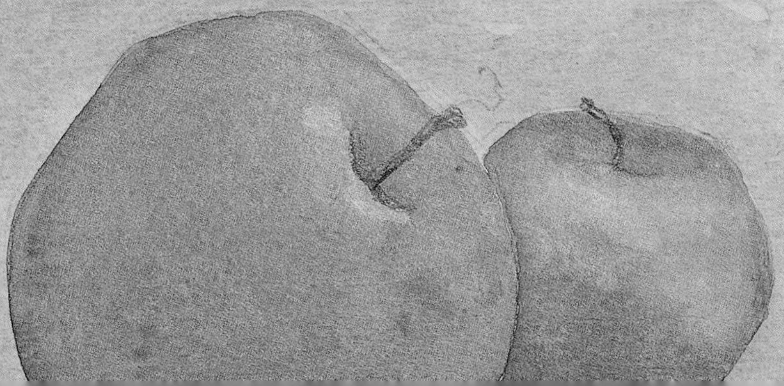

Isaac still said nothing.

Isaac didn't know what to say.

He did not have any friends.
He had never helped anyone and, until now,
no one had ever helped him.

He liked being on his own.

He turned around
and walked back to
his pile of leaves.

He was just getting comfortable when...

THUD!

Isaac looked at
the apple.

He thought about
the donkey.

He thought about how
the donkey couldn’t
reach the apples.

And then he thought,
perhaps...

Perhaps being alone isn't
so great after all.

For Ol, who cooked & Cai, who slept ~